Pig Kahuna

PIRATES!

Jennifer Sattler

W9-BYD-916

SCHOLASTIC INC.

No part of this publication may be reproduced, stored in a retrieval system,
or transmitted in any form or by any means, electronic, mechanical, photocopying,
recording, or otherwise, without written permission of the publisher.
For information regarding permission, write to
Bloomsbury Children's Books, 1385 Broadway, New York, NY 10018.

ISBN 978-0-545-75187-2

Copyright © 2014 by Jennifer Sattler. All rights reserved.
Published by Scholastic Inc., 557 Broadway, New York, NY 10012,
by arrangement with Bloomsbury Children's Books.
SCHOLASTIC and associated logos are trademarks and/or registered trademarks of Scholastic Inc.

12 11 10 9 8 7 6 5 4 3 2 1   15 16 17 18 19 20/0

Printed in the U.S.A.   08

This edition first printing, January 2015

Art created with acrylics and colored pencil
Typeset in Birdlegs
Book design by Nicole Gastonguay

For Bob Barnes

It was Sunday. Dink had just woken
up from his nap, grumpy and all out
of sorts.

His big brother, Fergus,

suggested they go for a dip.

But it was *t-t-too c-c-cold!*

Fergus had another idea. "How about some castle building?"

Dink tried, but every time he got started, a mean ol' wave would wash his castle away.

Usually a snack and a juice box
made Dink one happy little piglet.

But not today.

"Fergus! Your digging ruined my snack!"
Dink said, spitting out sand from his mouth.

He was so upset he threw his juice box.

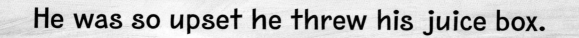

"Dink!" cried Fergus. "This hole is not a trash can."

"Well," Dink answered, pointing, "what's THAT, then?"

A pirate hat!

Fergus was inspired.

He got right to work building
a pirate ship out of sand.

Dink thought it looked like fun.

But he didn't really know
how to help.

As the ship got better
and better . . .

Dink's mood got worse . . .

. . . and worse.

It's hard to build a pirate ship when you're having a temper tantrum.

It's also hard to
finish your snack.

Or take a walk.

And when a crab snapped
him on the toe . . .

"Shiver me timbers!" yelled Fergus.

"You're a perfect pirate, Dink! You even have the stink eye!"

"I am?" asked Dink. "I do?"

Fergus nodded.

He placed the pirate hat on Dink's head.

The two brothers took their
places onboard the ship.

Fergus saluted, shouting,
"I saw a sea monster
headed that way, Captain!"

"Aaarrrgh!"

Digging in the sand can lead to

all kinds of buried treasure . . .

www.scholastic.com

Cover illustrations © 2014 by Jennifer Sattler
This edition is available for distribution only through the school market.

ISBN 978-0-545-75187-2 $4.99